Team Stats—Basketball Edition

NEW YORK KNICKS

Nicki Clausen-Grace
and Jeff Grace

BLACK RABBIT BOOKS

Bolt is published by Black Rabbit Books
P.O. Box 3263, Mankato, Minnesota, 56002.
www.blackrabbitbooks.com

Jennifer Besel, editor; Michael Sellner, designer;
Omay Ayres, photo researcher

Library of Congress Cataloging-in-Publication Data
Names: Clausen-Grace, Nicki, author. | Grace, Jeff, author.
Title: New York Knicks / by Nicki Clausen-Grace and Jeff Grace.
Description: Mankato, Minnesota : Black Rabbit Books, [2021] |
Series: Bolt. team stats-basketball edition | Includes bibliographical references and index. | Audience: Ages 8-12 | Audience: Grades 4-6 |
Summary: "Discover the New York Knicks' powerhouse players and biggest moments through exciting text and dynamic infographics"— Provided by publisher.
Identifiers: LCCN 2019051128 (print) | LCCN 2019051129 (ebook) |
ISBN 9781623102944 (hardcover) | ISBN 9781644663905 (paperback) |
ISBN 9781623103880 (ebook)
Subjects: LCSH: New York Knickerbockers (Basketball team)—Juvenile literature. | Basketball—New York (State)—New York—Juvenile literature. | Basketball players—United States—Juvenile literature.
Classification: LCC GV885.52.N4 C53 2021 (print) | LCC GV885.52.N4 (ebook) | DDC 796.323/64097471—dc23
LC record available at https://lccn.loc.gov/2019051128
LC ebook record available at https://lccn.loc.gov/2019051129

Printed in the United States. 2/20

All facts and statistics are current as of the 2018–2019 season.

Image Credits

AP Images: ASSOCIATED PRESS, 19, 22; Bill Kostroun, 10–11; Ed Kolenovsky, 28–29; Kathy Willens, Cover; Marty Lederhandler, 24; MICHAEL CONROY, 12; Ron Frehm, 15, 18; bleacherreport.com: Bleacher Report, 4–5; commons.wikimedia.org: Library of Congress Prints and Photographs Division., 7; Dreamstime: Gabriel Robledo, 3, 8; ESNY: Danny Small, 20–21; Getty: New York Daily News Archive, 16–17, 19, 23; New York Post Archives, 4–5; Orlando Sentinel, 26–27; Newscom: SportsChrome, 21; Shutterstock: Duda Vasilii, 28–29; EFKS, Cover, 1; GOLFX, 31; IfH, Cover; vasosh, 17, 25, 28–29, 32; SocImages: Lisa Wade, 7

CONTENTS

CHAPTER 1
On the Court. 5

CHAPTER 2
History of the Knicks. .6

CHAPTER 3
Greatest Moments. . . .10

CHAPTER 4
Knicks Superstars. . . .18

Other Resources. 30

On the COURT

It was the 1970 NBA Finals. The New York Knicks played the Los Angeles Lakers. Willis Reed, Knicks team captain, was injured. As players warmed up for Game 7, Reed limped onto the court. The crowd went wild. He scored the first two baskets in the game. His leadership **inspired** his team. The Knicks won the game and its first championship.

CHAPTER 2

History of the KNICKS

New Yorkers have loved the Knicks since it formed in 1946. It is one of the oldest NBA teams. Its fans are loyal, even though it's only won two championships. The Boston Celtics started the same year as the Knicks. That team has 17 titles.

1946 team

Knick is short for "knickerbockers." Dutch settlers wore knickerbocker pants in the 1600s. Dutch people settled New York. The name honors that history.

Teams Worth the Most Money

(as of 2018)

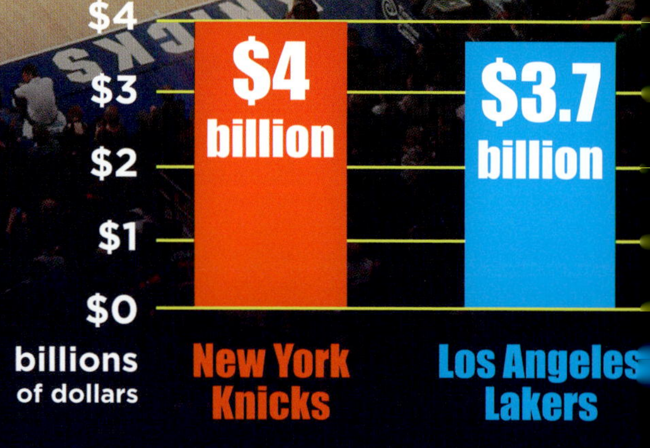

Big Money

The Knicks team is a big winner at the bank. The team was worth $4 billion in 2018. That was more than any other team. Teams make money in many ways. They sell tickets and **souvenirs** at games. Companies pay to **sponsor** teams. Teams also get money for being on TV.

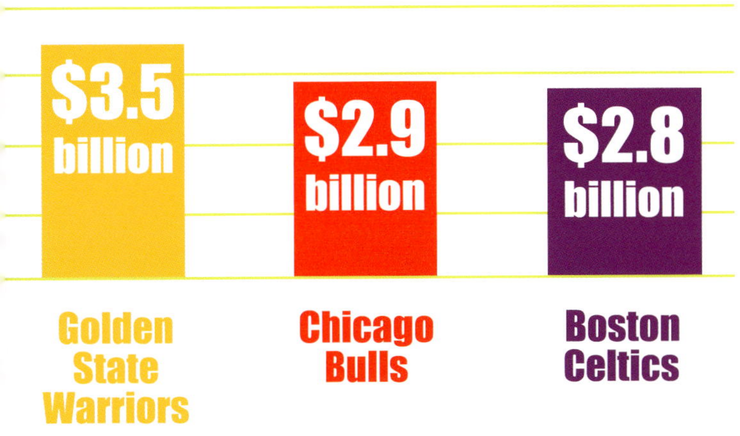

CHAPTER 3

Greatest MOMENTS

Big, exciting action keeps Knicks fans happy. In 2014, the team played the Charlotte Bobcats. Time was running out in the first half. Carmelo Anthony shot from almost half court. And he made it! Anthony ended the first half with 37 points. He went on to score 62 points in the game. That performance set a Knicks record. It's the most points a player has scored in a game.

NEW YORK
7
NEW YORK
7

The eighth seed plays the first seed in the first round. The eighth seed usually loses.

Coming from Behind

In the 1999 **playoffs**, the team was definitely an underdog. It was the eighth **seed**. And it wasn't expected to go past the first round. But the players fought hard. They beat the Miami Heat in the first round. In the semifinals, they destroyed the Atlanta Hawks. Then they won the Eastern Conference Finals. No one could believe it. The Knicks became the first eighth seed to go to the NBA Finals.

Getting to the Finals

Game 7 of the 1994 Eastern Conference Finals was important. The Knicks faced the Indiana Pacers. The winner would go to the Finals. The Knicks trailed by one point with 34 seconds left. Knicks player John Starks missed a layup. Teammate Patrick Ewing got the rebound. He scored and helped the Knicks to victory.

NBA
EWING
33
WORKMAN
3

Knicks Team Records

By the Numbers

60

most **wins** in a season

130–82

score of biggest **win**

100–162

score of biggest **loss**

152
most points
scored in
a game
17 fewest
wins
in a season
45 fewest
points
scored
in a game

CHAPTER 4

KNICKS Superstars

Great coaches and players draw in fans. To help it win, the Knicks has brought in many head coaches. In fact, the team has had 29 different coaches. Red Holzman coached the team for 14 seasons. He led it to both its NBA titles.

Knicks Coaches with the Most Wins

RED HOLZMAN
613 games won

JEFF VAN GUNDY
248 games won

JOE LAPCHICK
326 games won

Patrick Ewing

Patrick Ewing is number one in many ways. He holds the Knicks record for most games played. He also scored the most **career** points. He has the most rebounds too.

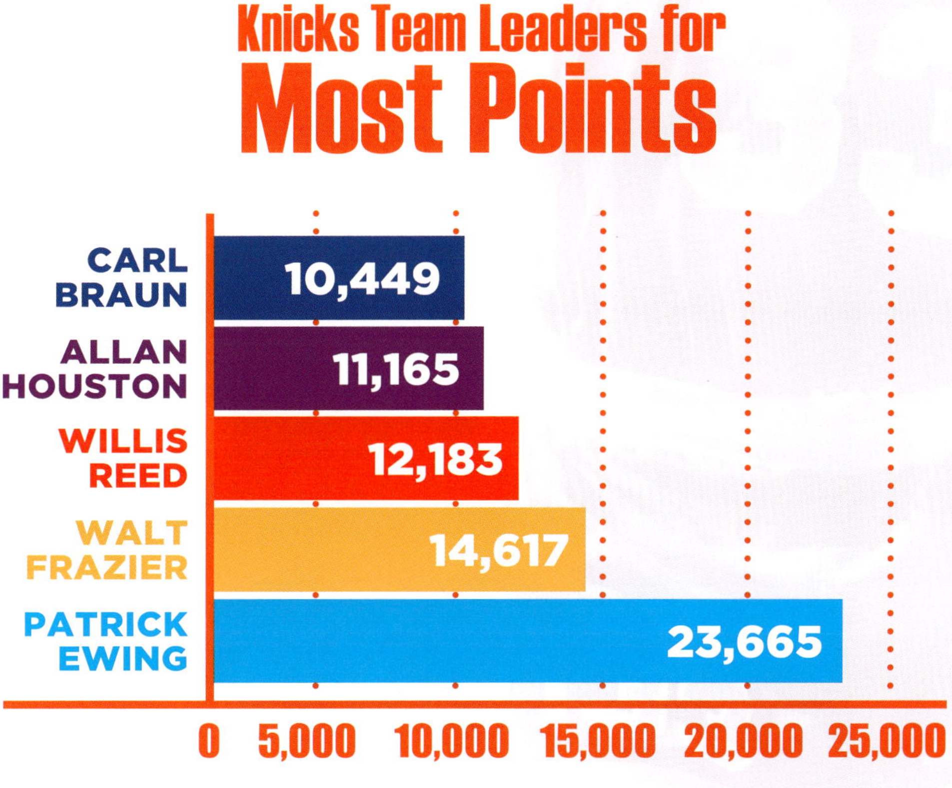

Willis Reed

Willis Reed played all of his 10 seasons with the Knicks. He **averaged** 18.7 points and 12.9 rebounds per game. He was on the team both times it won the championship.

The year 1970 was great for Reed. He was named MVP for the All-Star Game. He was the NBA MVP. He was also the Finals MVP. He was the first player to win all these awards in one year.

NEW YORK
19
50
10

MILWAUKEE
Walt Frazier

Walt Frazier

Walt Frazier was known for his great **defense** and fast hands. He was always willing to pass the ball. He said it was better than taking a bad shot. Frazier won two NBA titles with the Knicks.

Carmelo Anthony

Carmelo Anthony was another powerful player. In seven seasons with the team, he averaged 24.7 points per game. The team paid him well for that power. In his last Knicks season, he earned about $332,000 per game.

The Knicks may not have the most championships. But it does have great players and loyal fans. For any team, that's a winning combination.

NEW YORK
7

KNICKS TIMELINE

1946

The team forms.

1970

Team wins its first NBA championship.

1973

Knicks win its second NBA championship.

1994

Team makes it to the NBA Finals.

1999

Knicks make it to the Finals again.

2014

Anthony scores 62 points in a game.

GLOSSARY

average (AHV-rij)—a number that is calculated by adding quantities together and then dividing the total by the number of quantities

career (kuh-REER)—a period of time spent in a job

defense (DEE-fens)—the act of trying to stop the other team from scoring

inspire (in-SPIHR)—to make someone want to do something

playoff (PLAY-ahf)—a series of games played after the regular season to decide which player or team is the champion

seed (SEED)—a player or team that is ranked as one of the best in a competition in order to be sure that the best players or teams do not play against each other in the early part of the competition

souvenir (SOO-veh-neer)—something kept as a reminder

sponsor (SPAHN-sur)—to pay the cost of an activity or event in return for the right to advertise during the activity or event

BOOKS

Anderson, Josh, and Heather Kissock. *New York Knicks.* Inside the NBA. New York: AV2 by Weigl, 2016.

Gigliotti, Jim. *New York Knicks.* Insider's Guide to Pro Basketball. Child's World: Mankato, MN, 2019.

Goodman, Michael E. *New York Knicks.* NBA Champions. Mankato, MN: Creative Education, 2018.

WEBSITES

Basketball
www.ducksters.com/sports/basketball.php

New York Knicks
www.britannica.com/topic/New-York-Knicks

New York Knicks
www.nba.com/knicks/

INDEX

A

Anthony, Carmelo, 10, 26, 29

E

Ewing, Patrick, 14, 21

F

formation, 6, 7, 28

Frazier, Walt, 21, 25

H

Holzman, Red, 18, 19

N

NBA championships, 5, 6, 18, 22, 25, 26, 28

NBA Finals, 5, 13, 14, 22, 29

net worth, 8–9

R

Reed, Willis, 5, 21, 22